For Harry, with love ~ M. C. B.

To my nephew, Luke Richard Wernert ~ T. M.

This edition published for Tangerine Press, an imprint of
Scholastic Inc., 557 Broadway; New York, NY 10012

Library of Congress Catalog Card Number available

Original edition published in English by Little Tiger Press,
an imprint of Magi Publications, London, England 2008

ISBN-10: 1-84506-942-0

ISBN-13: 978-1-84506-942-1

Printed in China

Library of Congress Cataloging-in-Publication Data is available for this title

One Rainy Day

M. Christina Butler

Illustrated by Tina Macnaughton

Pitter-pat! Pitter-patter, pitter-pat!

Little Hedgehog woke up to the sound
of raindrops. "Hooray!" he cried happily.
"It's raining at last! I can wear my new
raincoat, hat, and boots and try out my
new umbrella."

Little Hedgehog wriggled
into his shiny new boots
as quickly as he could.
He ran outside and
opened his umbrella
with a *pop*!

Pitter-patter, pitter-pat!
The raindrops bounced
all around him.

"This is great!" Little Hedgehog laughed, spinning the umbrella around and around and splashing in the deepest puddle he could find.

"Is there room under that umbrella for me?" came Mole's small voice from nearby. "I'm getting very wet out here."

"My goodness! You *are* wet, Mole! Here,
take my umbrella," said Little Hedgehog.
"What are you doing out in the rain?"

"My house is full of water," replied Mole
sadly, "and I'm looking for somewhere to
dig a new home."

"I'll come and help you!" Little
Hedgehog offered.

"Thank you!" said Mole, smiling.

Mole snuggled under the umbrella and danced down the path in front of Little Hedgehog. Then, all at once, a gust of wind turned the umbrella inside out. Little Hedgehog raced after Mole as he was swept off the ground.

"*Help!*" cried Mole. "Little
Hedgehog! Help!"
"I've got you!" yelled
Little Hedgehog, holding
on to Mole's feet.

Little Hedgehog
pulled with all his
might. They wibbled
and they wobbled, and then they
both fell over . . . **BUMP!**

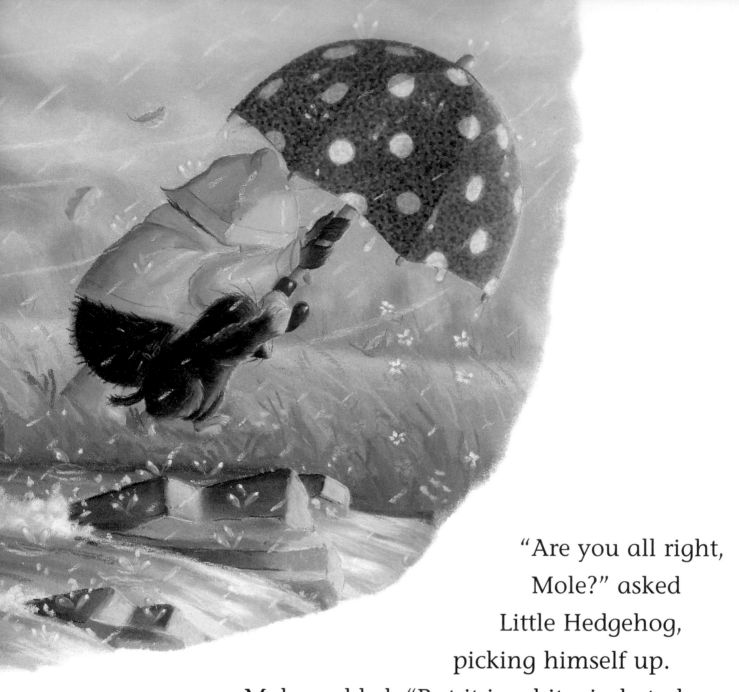

"Are you all right,
Mole?" asked
Little Hedgehog,
picking himself up.
Mole nodded. "But it is a bit windy today.
Can we look for my new home tomorrow?"
"Good idea," replied Little Hedgehog. "We'll go
back to my house and try again in the morning."

But just when they thought
the wind had passed, a huge gust
tossed them like autumn leaves
high into the air.

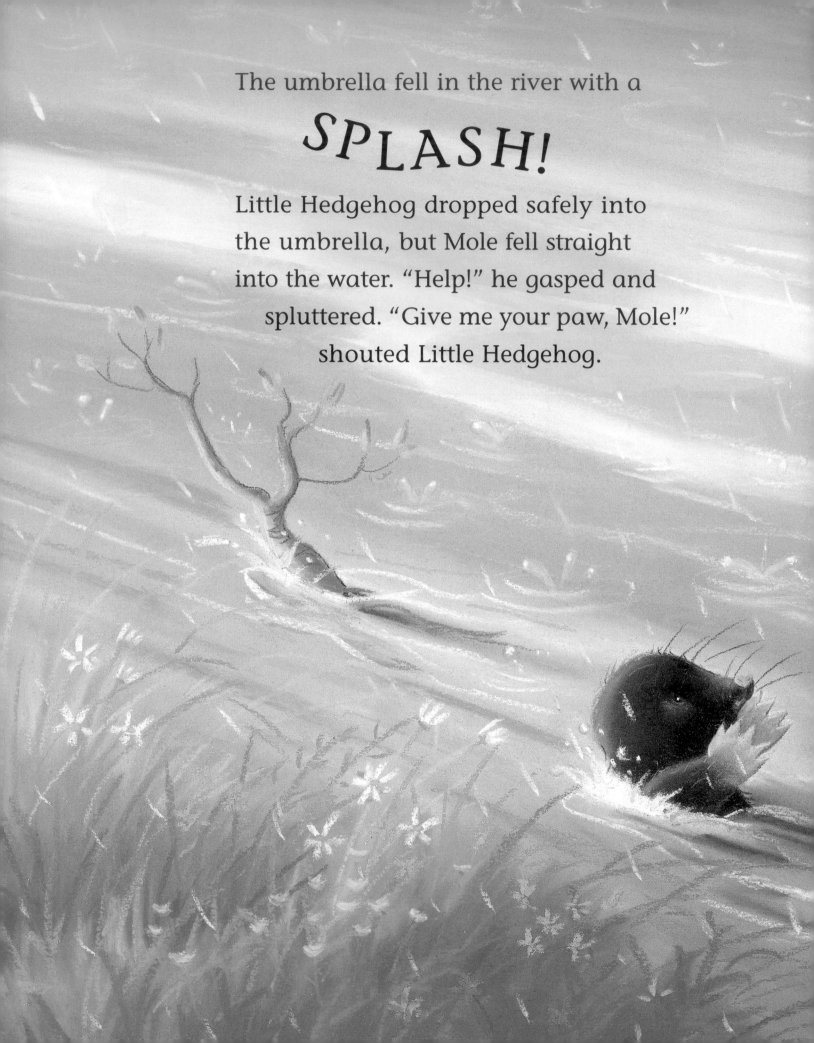

The umbrella fell in the river with a

SPLASH!

Little Hedgehog dropped safely into
the umbrella, but Mole fell straight
into the water. "Help!" he gasped and
spluttered. "Give me your paw, Mole!"
shouted Little Hedgehog.

Mole scrambled into the umbrella as it
bobbed on its way down the river.

"Thank you, Little Hedgehog," he
whispered, shivering, but then he sat up.
"I can hear someone shouting!" It was Fox,
waving from the bank.

"Over there!" yelled Fox, pointing. "Mouse and her family are trapped! The water is flooding the meadow. Can you rescue them?"

"Come on, Mole!" said Little Hedgehog. "Let's go!"

He pulled two sticks from the river and, with Mole's help, paddled the umbrella boat across to the mice.

The water was getting higher and higher.
   "We're coming!" called Little Hedgehog
as the frightened mice swung back and
forth on the grass.

Then, one by one, he and Mole
lifted Mother Mouse and her
babies gently into the umbrella.

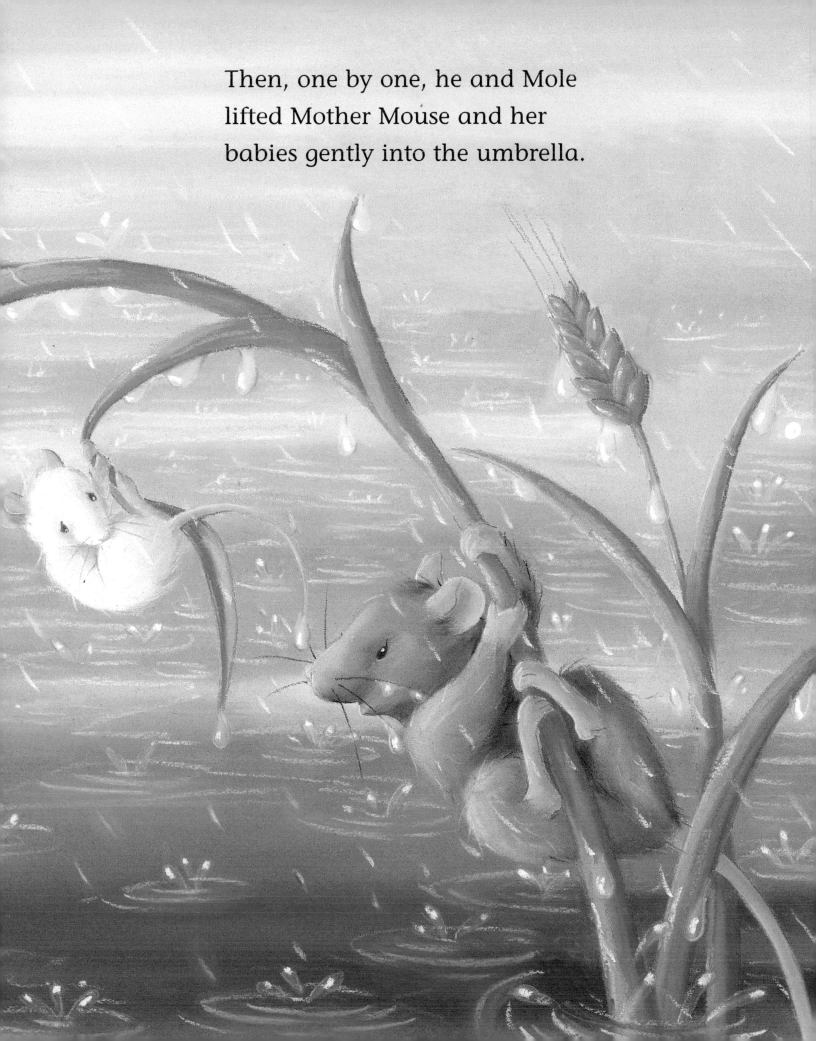

Twisting and turning
on the swirling waters,
Little Hedgehog and
Mole paddled hard
toward the safety
of the bank.

"Safe and sound," said Fox, helping them out.
"Let's go to Badger's house to
 dry off."

When they arrived
they found Badger
very grumpy.
    "You'd think
there was plenty of
room outside for the
rain without it coming
through my roof!" he
snapped, watching the water
drip, drip, drip onto his floor.

But Little Hedgehog
had a wonderful
idea . . . .

He opened his umbrella and pushed it through the roof, so the umbrella caught all the drips!

"Splendid!" cried Badger. "Three cheers for Little Hedgehog! And now let's have some cocoa."

So, warm and dry, the friends curled up by the fire and told Badger all about their rainy day!